Daniel's Potty Time

Adapted by Alexandra Cassel Schwartz
Based on the episode "Daniel Doesn't Want to Go Potty"
written by Syndi Shumer
Poses and layouts by Jason Fruchter

SIMON SPOTLIGHT
An imprint of Simon & Schuster Children's Publishing Division • New York London Toronto Sydney New Delhi
1230 Avenue of the Americas, New York, New York 10020 • This Simon Spotlight edition August 2019
For information about special discounts for bulk purchases, please contact Simon & Schuster Special Sales at
1-866-506-1949 or business@simonandschsuter.com. • Manufactured in the United States of America 0822 LAK
6 7 8 9 10 • ISBN 978-1-5344-5175-9 • ISBN 978-1-5344-5176-6 (eBook)

"Hi, neighbor!" said Daniel Tiger. "We're meeting Katerina at the market today. We're going to pick up toppings and make veggie pizza!"

"You should try to go potty before you leave the house," said Mom Tiger.

"I don't have to go potty," replied Daniel. He just wanted to go meet Katerina.

"Okay," said Mom. "But remember, there's no potty on Trolley!"

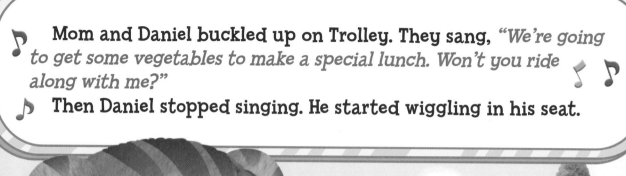

♪ Mom and Daniel buckled up on Trolley. They sang, *"We're going to get some vegetables to make a special lunch. Won't you ride along with me?"*

♪ Then Daniel stopped singing. He started wiggling in his seat.

Daniel realized that he needed to go potty. But there was no potty on Trolley!

"We'll have to stop, turn around, and go back home," said Mom.

"But Katerina is waiting for us at the market." Daniel was worried. "What if she leaves?"

"The most important thing right now is to listen to your body," said Mom. Then she sang, *"Do you have to go potty? Maybe yes. Maybe no. Why don't you sit and try to go?"*

"Okay, I will do that!" said Daniel.

Once they got home, Daniel went to the potty. He wasn't sure if he was done yet, so he sang, *"Do you have to go potty? Maybe yes. Maybe no. Why don't you sit and try to go?"*

Daniel sat and waited some more.

While he waited, Daniel played an I Spy game!

I spy with my tiger eye something with a big blue tail: my whale!

I spy with my tiger eye something that stays afloat: my boat!

I spy with my tiger eye something that can make me clean: the soap!

Daniel wiped, flushed, and washed his hands. Then he was on his way! "Now we can head to the market," said Mom.

"But, Mom," said Daniel, "*you* didn't go to the potty! *Do you* ♪ ♪ *have to go potty? Maybe yes. Maybe no. Why don't you sit and try to go* . . . *because there's no potty on Trolley!*"

Mom laughed. Daniel was right. She went to the potty too. Then they were ready to go to the market again.

When they got to the neighborhood market, Daniel couldn't find Katerina anywhere. "Maybe she went home," Daniel said sadly. Mom and Daniel decided to pick out the veggie pizza toppings before looking for Katerina at the treehouse.

Katerina was at the treehouse! "Hi, Katerina!" Daniel said. "Can you still come over for lunch?"

"Yes, meow meow!" Katerina replied. "Veggie pizza is so yummy-in-my-tummy!"

Once they arrived at Daniel's house, Daniel and Katerina ran into the kitchen to wash their hands. Mom Tiger rolled out the dough and spread the tomato sauce. Daniel sprinkled cheese and broccoli on top. Katerina added her favorite bell peppers.

Daniel wanted to keep cooking, but his tummy started to hurt. "When your tummy hurts, that might mean you need to go poop," Mom said. *"Do you have to go potty? Maybe yes. Maybe no. Why don't you sit and try to go?"*

Daniel waited on the potty. He did have to poop! Then he wiped, flushed, and washed his hands. He was ready to cook again!

The veggie pizza turned out deeelicious!
"Next time before you leave the house, you can try going to the potty too," said Daniel. "Ugga Mugga!"